12/13/05

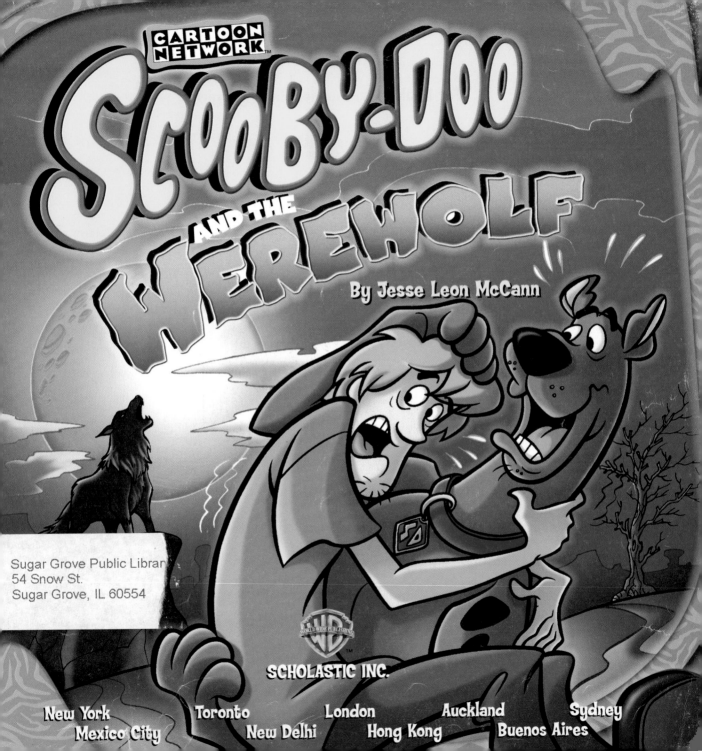

CARTOON NETWORK

# SCOOBY-DOO

### AND THE WEREWOLF

By Jesse Leon McCann

WB WORLDWIDE PUBLISHING

SCHOLASTIC INC.

New York    Toronto    London    Auckland    Sydney

Mexico City    New Delhi    Hong Kong    Buenos Aires

For Danielle and Ashley: Love ya, girls!

ISBN 0-439-45524-3

Copyright© 2004 by Hanna-Barbera.

Cover design by Louise Bova
Interior design by Amy Heinrich

12  11  10  9  8  7  6  5  4  3          4  5  6  7  8  9/0

Special thanks to Duendes del Sur for cover and interior illustrations.

Printed in the U.S.A.
First printing, September 2004

There was lots of excitement at Shaggy's house! An exchange student from Romania was coming to stay with Shaggy and Scooby-Doo. They didn't know anything about Romania, so Velma brought over some books for them to read.

"Zoinks!" cried Shaggy after Velma left. "That's a lot of books! Like, I've got a better idea, Scoob. Let's rent a video about Romania instead."

"Reah! Reah!" Scooby agreed. He licked his chops. Now he and Shaggy could eat popcorn and snacks and learn at the same time!

The movie the two friends rented told the story of a young man from Romania who was cursed by a gypsy. Every time the autumn moon rose, he would turn into a werewolf! The movie had a lot of spooky special effects. It was very scary!

The next day, the Mystery, Inc. gang went to the airport to pick up André, the Romanian exchange student. Shaggy and Scooby were a little nervous about André staying with them. After all, Romania was where werewolves came from!

When André got off the plane, Scooby-Doo and Shaggy turned cold with fear.

"Like, gee whiz, Scooby," Shaggy gulped. "Look how hairy André is!"

"Reah!" Scooby shivered. "Rairy rike a rererolf!"

7

Shaggy and Scooby-Doo worried all day long. What would happen after sunset, when the moon came out? It was September, an autumn moon. Fortunately, André retired to his room as soon as evening fell. Unfortunately, they found animal hairs all over the house! Were they from André?

Scooby and Shaggy couldn't sleep. Not when a werewolf might be staying in their house! They kept guard until midnight. Then they heard someone open and close the front door. It was André! He'd sneaked outside in the middle of the night!

Scooby and Shaggy were terrified. They didn't want to follow André! But they had to find out if he was a werewolf. So they quietly followed André into the night. And just when they saw him . . .

"Hoowwwwwrl!"

"Zoinks! He's howling at the moon, Scoob!" Shaggy whispered urgently. "And he's all hairy!"

"Roh ro!" Scooby was about to faint.

Scooby and Shaggy raced back home and hid under Shaggy's bed. They couldn't sleep a wink! Had André really turned into a werewolf?

Scooby and Shaggy knew they had to find out for sure. First thing in the morning, they went to an old bookstore. Way in the back were all the books about monsters. Shaggy read about werewolves – most important, how to tell if someone is one!

One book Shaggy read said that werewolves are driven away by a plant called wolfsbane. Luckily, there was a shop in town that sold it. Scooby and Shaggy took the wolfsbane home and showed it to André. André quickly excused himself and left the room!

13

Another book said that werewolves didn't like things made of silver. So Shaggy grabbed a silver spoon from the kitchen. When André wasn't expecting it, Shaggy and Scooby jumped out and held up the spoon. Sure enough, André turned away. Now they were certain that André was a werewolf!

Shaggy and Scooby needed to warn their friends. They knew Velma and Daphne would be over at Fred's house. As soon as André was out of the way, they slipped out. But they had a funny feeling they were being followed! Was it André?

"Like, run, Scoob!" Shaggy cried. "If André bites us, we'll be turned into werewolves, too!"

"Relp! Relp!" Scooby yelped. "Rye ron't rant ro re ra rererolf!"

They ran through the city as fast as their feet could carry them!

Scooby and Shaggy dashed through the baseball field and vacant lots, through the park and into back alleys. They were certain André was right behind them – and he was probably gaining on them!

Just when they thought they couldn't take another step, Shaggy pulled Scooby behind some trash cans. The creature behind them passed by without noticing them.

"Zoinks! That was close!" Shaggy panted. "C'mon, Scoob! Let's get to Fred's!"

"Relp! Relp! Rerewolf!" Scooby-Doo cried as he and Shaggy charged into Fred's house.

"Like, you've got to help us!" Shaggy hollered. "The werewolf may be right outside!"

"Jinkies! What are you guys talking about?" Velma frowned. "There's no such thing as werewolves!"

Just then, André walked out of the rest room.

"Like, it's him!" Shaggy shrieked. "He's the werewolf!"

"We invited André over for a nice dinner, not to be called a werewolf," Daphne said.

"Oh yeah?" Shaggy said. "If he's not a werewolf, then why did he turn furry and howl at the moon? Why did he leave hairs all over the house? And why did he run away when we brought out wolfsbane and silver? Huh? Huh?"

"Reah!" Scooby scowled suspiciously.

"I am so sorry," André said shyly. "My fur coat is getting very old. I am afraid it sheds."

"I howled at the moon because I was so very happy to be spending time in America, you see." André explained. "But I do not understand your customs here. Why did you wave weeds in my face? I am very allergic. And why did you use that spoon to reflect sunlight at me? It really hurt my eyes!"

"Like . . . because . . . uh . . . you're a . . . werewolf?" Shaggy said timidly.

"*Whew!* Sorry, André. Like, Scooby and I feel like first-class dunces!"
Shaggy sighed. "Right, Scoob?"

"Ruh-huh!" Scooby agreed.

"It is funny you thought I was a werewolf." André smiled. "Yet you
never asked which part of Romania I am from."

"I am from Transylvania!" André declared. "Home of the vampire!"
For a second, Shaggy and Scooby were scared stiff! Then they heard their friends laughing, and they knew André was just kidding. Soon everyone was laughing, cheering, and giving André a proper welcome. "Scooby-Dooby-Doo!" Scooby exclaimed.